CW01618922

THE WA ED

The Walking Wounded

RORY BRENNAN

DEDALUS

THE DEDALUS PRESS
46 Seabury, Sydney Parade Avenue, Sandymount, Dublin 4

© Rory Brennan 1985

ISBN 0 948268 09 3 (paper)
ISBN 0 948268 08 5 (bound)

ACKNOWLEDGEMENTS
Acknowledgements are due to the editors of the following journals in which some of these poems first appeared: The Irish Press, The Irish Times, Tracks, Poetry Ireland Review. The poem "Drives" won the William Allingham Award in 1983.

All rights reserved.

Grant-aided by The Arts Council.

Typesetting & make-up: Vermilion
Cover design: Brendan Foreman

Contents

for Lally and Olive

THE WALKING WOUNDED

In the lace curtain of old newsreels
They manage to force a grin through burnt-cork lips
And sketch a wave with a soaking stump,
Almost manic in their terrible turbans.
Only the blind can ignore the peeping lens
And the deafened will never hear the sleek
Commentator so plausibly vaunt their wounds.
Only a flicker endures of all their pain.

Time and again I am drawn into the fine mesh
Of their memory. In the graven dream of an action replay
I can see them stumble in slow motion along a road
Away from the battle, their arms around each other.
Such terrible things are needed to make us tender.
Even we know this, who have never fought save in
Love's long war of attrition, and we also know
How the shadow of death so lightens a burdened sky.

Today in the drizzle of Dublin I saw the round shoulders
Of their shadows fall like broken columns across the road.
Actium, Anzio, the shape of all the shattered legions is seen
In the dredging limp the self-mutilated make
On wet concrete that's the colour of their eyes, all those
Who signed the deed of their lives with an illegible scrawl.
I straighten up and feel myself unscathed. So tell me
What tugs at my tendons and webs the rim of my mouth?

INSULARITIES

A tideless sea needs turbulence.
A breath of air sandpapering
The laquered woodgrain
Is not enough to bring relief
From fatal listlessness.
Masts on the horizon
Or low melting plumes
Hiss like a burning fuse.

So they built inland
Where the wind loudmouths
Each solid citizen or
Simpers in summer
Insinuatingly on certain streets
But never stops.
From up there the sea's
A blottingpad of cloud.

It sucked me once off Naxos
Where the swell seemed childsplay
Till the breakers smacked
The boat for giving cheek.
Buckling lungs were scoured
For air, and limbs were weed.
Slumped on the sand,
That hint life-humbled me.

Sunsets were made for cognac
Or vice versa — as you wish.
I like sometimes to sip alone
Conjuring old friends in café chairs
And wait until the winestained
Rug unrolls itself across
The sagging tongued and grooved
To top my sinking glass.

Two winters my drenched window
Saw the sea cast fish-hooks
From a wedge of rocks.
Still frozen, the spray particles
Hang lucidly at night,
Barbed, unassailable yet falling
Through my becalmed sleep
Into the troubled breathing of the sea.

LEONARDO'S CREW

The echo-sounder, a bad artist,
Sketched a Gothic seabed, crags and cliffs,
Surreal yet conceivable to us
Who'd sailed between the islands
And, although we'd heard no music,
Smelt the fear of death sweat fishslime
In the armpits of those hollowchested rocks
And coil up our nostrils like an octupus.

The serrated currents sawed the boat
Across the shoulderblade of bay again.
This time the sounder drew a plain and gulf
Where Leonardo knew to lay his labyrinth
Of nets already stacked like hives along the deck.
So close to life are the tough trades of death
We flatter them with talk of purity. Old
Andreas dealt the nets like cards across the stern.

The sun drained down his bottle, sprinkling dregs
Across the tasselled wake. In a soft fleece
Of air I ruled the flinching tiller towards the land.
Lobster, retsina, sleep. At dawn the water's entrails
To wind up. Andreas, Leonardo keep the wave's rough
Rhythm with the world. Theirs is the false cadence.
Crumpling across the bay that night we heard
In the sea's lung the cough of dynamite.

THE UNTOUCHABLE

The Himalays wore a sari of cloud
As we trekked through the foothills.
In a tiny village we met him — thin, shy,
Loitering like a pedlar with nothing to sell.
We showed by gestures we needed a bearer.
Without a word to anyone he came,
Shouldering silently the heaviest pack.
Forests were hedges on those mountainsides
That treat the sky as equal.
The six — now seven — of us trudged all day
As Annapurna held itself aloof.
We pushed on through the villages. Once
We stopped to gulp tea at a fly-blown stall —
But his cup was put on the ground before him.
He stooped and drank. Outraged, we flung
Our arms around him, yelled at the Indians —
Did our rupees make us touchable?
Weren't we, in their scheme of things, as low?
The locals giggled at the foreign fools.
For three nights he stayed and slept rough,
Then wandered off with his pay and a casual wave
As self-contained as the conquered mountains.

THE ARCHAEOLOGISTS

No scholar can quite carbon-date
Love's first strata in the soil
Or all its layers excavate
Although his workers delve and toil

Like council workers in a drain
For bone or terracotta shard.
To piece the jar back like a brain
Is slow surgery and hard

And from its shape to so deduce
A culture and a state of mind
Seems idle, as of little use
As love's lost artefacts to find

Once they're bulldozed beyond hope.
Still like tenacious scholars we
Read surface signs and scrape and grope,
Unearth our glinting treasury.

DRIVES

It was never noosed in the long necklace
Of catseyes that coiled us home those nights.
No, too nervous to trap much of easy peace
My father squinted into dipped headlights

And jerked us back across the Glenshane Pass,
Belfast-to-Derry, Ireland's lumpy throat.
Though once, parked on a pier, we shared a glass,
My mother sketching a net-shrouded boat.

In Sligo — for my sake — we visited Drumcliff.
Crows cawed like circling demons round the tower.
Life was the imitator I knew there and then. Grief
Keeps love's twisting mind from turning sour.

Now you and I who have travelled so many roads
Still point north at weekends, the children curled
Asleep on the back seat. Long distance moods
Mix with the marks of war. I steer my turning world.

THE KNIFE-THROWER'S PERSONAL RELATIONSHIPS

The blades cartwheel through the low beamed lights,
Is it a form of love that steadies his aim?

The drummer rattles out distant gunfire
As if a regiment were drawn up for an execution.

Thuds stake her out, breast, brain and thigh.
Forked and splayed she keeps a performer's smile

As he bowls his knives. How do they always
Land on the tip and not on the haft?

Sequined, she steps out from her stabbed cross.
Would you step in to face the whistling steel?

They bow and again we notice she is beautiful.
Applause swells in the tent like hoofbeats.

This is the act of faith turned professional.
And maybe sheer hate too governs his hand,

He will not give her the satisfaction of being slit open.
Think how we gut each other. Think of them.

ISTERNI SEQUENCE

A chessboard of pasture and ploughland,
Its pieces olive tress, lime cubes of light,
Those decimated bales are captured pawns,
The harvest's nearly in, these last few moves,
Three ringworm wells, bulb of a local church . . .
A landscape cannot move . . . but it can change.
Stalemated on this empty square I know
My plotted games were played against myself.

Rough red was sunset in the afternoon,
Rolled blood inside the flashing toasting glass.
We left the vineshade for this clicking hill
Where chainsaw crickets saw siestas through
And found three fractured rooms, bones
Of old porous beams and bamboo veins,
Multiple wounds with scales of brittle mud,
The leavings of this house hung on its rack.

The verb to house, we use it for our hopes.
Take from the well. The path is like a torrent,
Only stone. Gush, rivulet and pool with
Weed for froth. Climbing against its current
With two toppling cans in merciless July
I've cursed each rut and buckle of its course,
Begrudged my mortgaged sweat on this mad house.
Hope drives the will to make a thing complete.

New beams bear the roof on rebuilt walls.
The weathered stones of language bend me now
To build more spacious rooms. The clotted
World has stemmed its haemorrhage. I prize
This contact with a false respite. Up here,
Where mules bring up supplies, they reap
The thinning hair of corn with sickles, bent
To a labour old and harsh as verse.

Tangling like lifelines the gnarled tracks
Entrench the hills. No shard-sprouting ground,
But there I found this handaxe. Cleanshaven stone,
Its thin serrated edge a small fish-mouth.
My own hand swallowed it. The dizzy space
Since someone held it shocked, a quiver
Of long continuity with another settling-down
Here where the Greeks call place of cisterns, Isterni.

After the doldrum heat when the Fortuna
Beats the patched carpet of the valley clean
It leaps to whip the pages of my book
Through snatching fingers. So years are grasped at
And as this one swivels on the ferry's prow
I walk back down the deck to watch the island
Shrink into an artist's model of itself. It shrinks
Until it's like a target in the rifled wake.

Ten Sketches from a Greek Terrace

1. THE OIL LAMP

I hear the bamboo creak like a cracked joint
Although the terrace stays so still-life still.
The oil lamp's blade is pared to a fine point
And purrs inside its glass. A long tendril
Wavers like a signal from its clouded stack.
The crickets tune non-stop their lost waveband
Deciphering a code they cannot crack
With only one glazed star to lend a hand . . .
A still scenario a good painter could
Catch all the silence in but not that creak
That has the nervy twang of brittle wood.
With a deep breath the decamped wind is back.
I look in at the window with a start:
The lantern's blade is jabbing at my heart.

2. THE THRESHING CIRCLES

It seems as if a giant coin was flipped
And spun three times, striking the hill
And stamping it with stone lipped
Perfect circles as it plunged and fell.
Miniature ring forts with broken teeth
For ramparts, trampling their floors
Horses in late summer churn a froth
Of chaff, a tent of golden filings in the air
To shelter them, gone absent without leave
From the massed ranks of myth. At night
The threshing circles rise again, have
Three counterparts that spatter light,
The bracelets of three villages that make
Circles like camp fires or birthday cakes.

3. THE ROCK SHRINE

A gate swings open like a broken wing
Into its sanctuary. Cleft more than cave,
A scoop of stone, its yawning overhang
The jaw that swallowed Jonah, or Christ's grave
If there was a huge rock to push across.
But it's so tranquil there in front of all
The make-do offerings, a cracked St Nicholas,
Dried flowers in a tincan incense bowl,
Small embossed limbs ribboned on rusty nails,
Direct requests and ruling out confusion
Should a saint slip up. Like the old gods
These iconed heads are seen as semi-human,
Fallible, knowing that faith demands we fail
And count on them against the loaded odds.

4. THE CISTERNS

To keep wells pure they tip in watersnakes.
Or so they say. I never saw one slink
Around the telescoped dark lakes
As I heaved buckets to the thirsty brink.
But it was cistern water that made empires great,
Let them, like us, survive the summer's seige
When more assailled them too, like us, than heat.
I raise a glass to them across an age —
Roman, Venetian, Turk — who slaked their thirst
For a few hundred years and spent
Their prime on a stump of castle, a smashed pier,
A few rocks blended with the landscape, lost.
Down I go to clean the tank each year.
Inside its head I slosh up sediment.

5. THE KESTREL

The world is art through strong binoculars,
Far nearer and remote, a film, untouchable
Though an arm's length away, and like the stars
That shimmer in the lens, so can the kestrel
Batten down the air to plane and hold
The wind back like a finger in a dyke of sky.
When the stalled heat starts turning cold
Out comes this bird that climbs to spy
The closecropped earth, the bush-daubed hills
For snakes and mice, a hedge-hopping surgeon
Than can slit and stitch, an invisible
Mender of the threadbare fields. Poised on a power-line
The kestrel appears urban and uninteresting,
No graph or signature in that shut wing.

6. THE ABANDONED FARMS

From Lesbos to the Blaskets it's not hard to find
Roofless cottages explaining the scrapped hulks
Of trawler or caique listing on the sand,
A seized crane and a mine of tackle
Venomous with rust their field-gun monument.
History files this under the Marshall Plan
When plentiful labour in the cities meant
The chop for subsistence farmer, fisherman,
An old folks home in every dwindling village.
Yes, yes, nostalgia's cheap — try hauling a clogged net
Or hoeing iron earth. The old here were the last
To break their backs. The land's worth money now. Yet
Only a fool would wish them back their past,
Only another this dismantled age.

7. THE LOCAL SAINTS

Littering the valleys, sprinkling the headlands
The small churches are spent cartridges,
Cylindrical though white instead of red
Or slanting into hills like a blunt wedge.
Each family has one where on the saint's day
They hold a festival, six hours of chanting prayer
Followed by a feast — these people pay
For pieties with revelry. What I love is the interior,
Long, cool and bare, a whiff of must and spice,
A sense of trespass even if you light
A beeswax votive candle or a wick
That floats on olive oil in an old glass.
Tin-framed and mildewed, shrunken, ascetic,
The old Byzantine saints are sitting tight.

8. THE LIZARD

He's two inches long. In a blow-up he'd be
A Hollywood monster from Planet of Dinosaurs,
Which is how he must seem to ant or flea.
Fast as a flashlight beam he slithers
From plaster crack to crevice over door
Or tries the North Face of the window frame,
A prehistoric micro-mountaineer
To a Woolworth design, transparent-plastic-brown.
But it's his little bloodshot pickled eye,
Cliffhanging in the bamboo-runnelled roof
That fixes and fixates me, so diamanté,
Merciless. He flicks his flick-knife
Tongue, impales, after a dogfight, a long legged fly.
I hear that tiny scuffle magnify.

9. OBJETS TROUVÉS

We keep too much. Houses can equal heads
For cluttered attics, chests whose drawers
Are jammed with out of date and awkward
Junk. There's no such problem here. Here
Different things accrue, we beachcomb them
Or pluck them from ploughed fields in early spring.
A niche in my study is their small museum.
A marble pestle, loomweights on a string,
A fragment with a figure on a horse worn
Ricepaper thin, a stamp franked by millenia,
Escaped, I swear, from Keats' heartbreaking urn.
Who sank with that encrusted amphora?
Or broke this sea-green glass, so sanded by the ocean
It's now a frosted pebble in my palm?

10. THE OTHER ISLANDS

Are mostly never there. A mosquito net of haze
Hangs loose offshore and wraps us lazily
In a steam bath horizon. It takes a blaze
Of sun in a stripped bare sky to see
The other mountain tops beyond our own
And be surprised again how self-contained
It's possible to be, or that to be alone
We can take too easily for granted like a friend.
I do not know their names — they end in -os
And certainly have favourite gods and crops,
A port and inland villages, places to visit,
Places I may have been — I need a map
Because I take on trust what lies so close
And for a change feel no strong need to name it.

PROGRAMME NOTE

Such shadows in that sound.
As you grew deaf
Your music darkened
Like a fist of cloud
Clenching for thunder.

Then through it like a laser beam
A scream as if the bow
Was disembowelling the violin.
That was the sound, the final
Sound of syphilis.

You were sacked from the State Opera,
Unable to conduct. Still that sound
Pulled barbed wire through your head.
Just before death
An overture of silence
Spilt like ointment in your ears.

A CHILD WITNESSES A DOMESTIC ROW

The lovely people she depends on
Are splintering the world with screams,
Catapulting each other with pellets of hate.

Secrets sifted through the membranes
Of soft intimacy are slung, and boomerang
In ragged volleys of scorn, grapeshot of spite.

Their mouths are twisted like torn pockets.
The child only hears the schoolyard words
Piledriving stakes into her foundation.

Under all the hammering a bit of her mind
Chips off, a stonemason's shard
Or sculptor's slip, a slice of stone

To be swept up like a bit of broken saucer.
No matter how shaved and sanded afterwards
That flaw describes the shape she will never have.

PUNK-ROCK REPUBLICAN

Punk-rock republican,
Pop croppy-boy,
Lime green and luminous
Your shirt and socks
Flash like flintlocks in
A psychedelic lithograph.
Whiteboy in bootboy boots
Your old man's braces hold
Your half-mast trousers up.
A pig, a paddy-pusher
Growls in quadrophonic
To a binlid beat.
Make shapes, man, shapes,
This is the History Disco.
Shamrocker Rule O.K.

ZERO OUTSIDE

For a deaf and dumb itinerant of eighteen, frozen to death outside his family caravan.

Dead livestock hit the headlines and
Hypothermia is almost fashionable.
Wrap up the old in tinfoil,
The radio doctor says.
Boil snow for water and —
Don't forget to feed the birds!
The news shows skiers and snowballing kids
Then shots of helicopters as they sling out bales
To huddling cattle. Diesel
Is frozen: milk froths on the snow.
The country slowly seizes up
And politicians burst like pipes.

But the climate was always hostile
For you and the likes of you.
Like ice on the window
Of a heated room
Your life seeped away.
This total silence suited us.

Cast in death, your body's mould
Is melting in the snowdrift with the thaw.
Old engines, batteries, dogshit, bones
Heap your scrapiron cairn.

THE WINDOW FOGGED

Mine was a childhood of high banked fires
In a well built house of big square rooms.
The window fogged before we pulled the curtains
And the radio held forth at half-past six

On things I'm not sure now if I really remember
Or read much later on. I played on the carpet
With soldiers of lead until tea came in
And we ate round a card table for a treat.

At the same time I could feel the stale breath
Of the poor and dowdy, the empty, the violent,
The world that was made of the other people on the bus,
The crowd in O'Connell Street, the noise outside the
    pubs,

And I always knew I would have to go very far
From the warm firelight of home. So often since then
I've needed every ounce of the gold-dust of love
And every ember of affection kindled there.

THE OLD RAZORS

Three generations of Gillette
Cohabit in the bathroom cabinet.
My grandfather's, entered
In a plush-lined stain-spotted
Silver case reflects a time
When lathering the face was still
Like setting fires or brewing tea
A sort of skill, domestic, leisurely.
His old razor's clawed, has teeth
Like solid talons.
Its head screws off. It has
The cruel air of a medical instrument.
A certain type of antique shop
Would snap it up. My grandfather
Must first have wielded it
When he was turning middle aged
And safety razors were the latest thing.

My father's is a screwbase job
Though you can see the family resemblance.
Also it's alloy, gleams
Dimly beside the elder generation.
I scraped my first
Unnecessary swathe with it.
Now there's no blade inside
Its long locked head
But it can cut me more.

Towel on shoulder,
His head a touch aslant,
In a steamy mirror
I see my father scrape
A Siberia of whiteness
From his death-stubbly face.

My own is swivel headed, double bladed
With a long ribbed stem for a handle.
How long will it last? I must
Have used and lost a dozen razors,
Forgotten in places I have forgotten.
In among the medicine bottles
The two relics are still serviceable.
How long will I last, is their
Aromatic question. They say,
You are losing your hair like one
Of our companion beaver brushes.
Don't be so smart, I say to them:
Soon there will only be disposables

SNOWBALL IN HELL

The russet wickerwork was leaking amber,
Lancing the whole leadveined nave
With silvery needles when the white pony

Emerged, muscle all flexing marble,
Stark as a wound against the buttressed trees.
We slowed to pass, our drumming cocoon

Churning the whiskey and burgundy leaves
And his head followed, pivoted so splendidly
The instant's privilege was etched forever.

A last long shot in the wing mirror
Held him astride the groin-vaulted road
Waiting to be straddled by a blood-flecked god —

A thought as stale as he is natural. Facts are
A boy from the tinker camp will saddle him up,
Sell him for trotting round a riding school.

MUTILATION

The day he wandered into the columned building —
So like the one where they'd sentenced him —
He was amazed the men in uniform let
Him past the polished doors. The humidifiers
Smelt of opulence. He fancied the well-
Dressed women strutting between the frames.
The ikons were useless; he liked battle scenes
And a few sleek black marble statues.
Mostly he hated the cool bright geometry
Of the Modern Wing. But he found her, sweet
And resplendent, in the Late Renaissance.
The madonna was so pure she was unreal;
The child was spoilt and adult, slightly smug,
And the saints had the air of mincing solicitors.
But she, she titillated shamelessly down in
The left-hand corner, smiling, accessible,
And kind. At first he'd thought the Gallery
Just a good place to keep warm. Now her
Nipples nibbled the lobes of his brain,
Maddened him nightly more than the most
Succulent centrefold. He bought a repro
Print and slobbered in adoration until
The solution sang clearer than any choir.
So the switchblade sprang and slashed
The sex-kitten angel's face. He gouged
And ripped the old master's mistress into shreds
While the attendants hung back terrified
And the alarm-bells screamed in celebration.

FADING TO TIME

For Tim Lehane

I float in a doubleglazed fishtank—
The walls are padded in purple hessian—
Waiting for a red light to let me speak.

In my ears a bedlam of schizoid angels
Flares and falls, a firework fanfare.
I have lucid moments when I hear voices.

Wire creepers with hairy protrusions
Drip from the ceiling. My life passes
Like rings narrowing on a turntable.

Lips fishmouth things, foreheads wrinkle up.
I feel the triple tapedeck is stacked against me.
So this is what it's like to be stonedeaf?

I turn off a second. Lights leap on. And
A familiar voice impersonates me as I talk
In amiable tones about history and art.

THE COUNTRY PARENTS

Glazing the wall a blue Paul Henry
Opens a window on a hardy childhood,
Thatch and turfstacks, Connemara
Kept like the Secred Heart, a family ikon.
Their lives were sucked smoothly as smoke
Into the tiled fireplace of a poky room,
For De Valera's rural dream was lived
In the strait-jacket of a semi-detached.

The Service, Customs, Banks, the National Schools,
Bled dry their mortgaged youth on tradesman's pay;
Promotion, the incremental scale, they cultivated
Like their patch of garden with its drill of spuds.
Regret manured the top-soil. They clung like clay
To the steady job while a million streamed
Down the pier with a few pence and a cardboard case
And the mailboat spat in its wake a trail of spittle.

No secretive tenantry hugged their acres closer
Though they lacked a flaunting landlord to execrate.
Each piece of furniture was an Act of Parliament
With Upper and Lower House as man and wife.
The priests approved with an air of slight disdain
And monitored their visits, no point in being too friendly
Where building funds cannot be properly buttressed.
They swallowed their medicine like altar wine.

With summer came the pilgrimage back to the small-
holding,
To a house soldiering on at the end of a rutted lane
Or back to a nest of rooms in a lopsided street,

The noises of a small town rattling in through the latch,
Back to the groundplan of childhood, where change is
charted
By absence, where the dead have willed little else but
their silence,
Acknowledgement of loss means never referring to all
You most care for. And all of this they took back to the
city.

No wonder their children reject like transplants
The withered ethic of duty and sacrifice
That made pebbles of their parents' hearts
And go wild or sullen on stout or smack.
The loutish pothead son with a failed degree,
The gymslipped child so suddenly a slut
Are creatures they cannot stand. Distress
Hangs like a kitchen smell at the foot of the stairs.

This city was never their home, only a lodging house
Between exile and inheritance, the cousin in Birmingham
And the family farm. Their place was to cheer in Croke
Park,
Their yells soaring like the hoarse shrapnel of crows.
Some grew to power greasing the cogs of money with
A will to work learned bullying at spiteful clay
But most just watched the dull play of their lives, not
learning
Places too will lie once they are not believed.

BUT GAELIC TOO

Leaving the Gaeltacht they labelled him
LONDON, slung like an animal collar around his neck.
Galway, Dublin, Holyhead. He got to Euston
Where a local from home took him up to Kilburn.
Next morning, the site. The foreman knew no Irish
Beyond *lámh, lámh eile,* which was all
That he wanted in any case. But he asked,
Have you a trade? Did you serve your time?
Are you a labourer? Poor spalpeen, victim
Of our apartheid, let's think for a second
How it took eighteen years of native culture
To produce the two English words you knew.
Nodding and grinning you just said: I dig.

FOURSOMES

1. HAMMOCK

He cut his ties. He didn't know it yet,
How severed rope unravels into string
That loops and knots into a subtler net.
When he lay back the sky began to swing.

2. CLOUDS FROM AN AIRCRAFT

Clouds from an aircraft float by lush
As snowdrifts. Night leaks into the sky
And the white dunes turn slowly into slush.
Partir? Mourir? Fasten your seatbelts. *Die!*

3. CHANGING TACK

The lunging cutlasses fall back
And panic strikes into the hangdog sails
That retch and quiver in the aimless slack
The way a hope, a gust of courage, fails.

4. THE LAST LAUGH

He always joked until it went too far.
The boat capsized. He did the anchor stroke.
The others swam and landed on the shore.
He got the point at last, but missed the joke.

THE STONE BOAT

When shipwrights first laid deeper keels
The medieval master builders saw
New transepts soar in the branching struts.
Under an early example in a Breton church
The slightly touched attendant
Showed us a stone boat — today a font —
A local saint had rowed across from Wales
With two straws for oars.
''Ne riez-pas!'' she suddenly snapped,
Long conditioned to tourist ridicule.
But we hadn't the ghost of a smile on our faces —
We Irish are used to improbable religion
And the things of God being often upside down.
Then she asked us for two francs each.

FAIL SAFE

I

He leapt three flights and lived.
In his chromium chair he cannot wink.
What snapped with his cortex?
No one really knows. The medics say
He hears his fellow patients' gibberish
As they build lego-bricks. So a pretty
Occupational therapist told me.

II

This one I have from an old poet.
He said she made absolutely
No mistake about it: a fist
Of sleeping pills and four
Stiff gins before the plunge
Into the swaying turning-nasty sea.

CULTURE ECLIPSE

Tinahealy 1981

All Wicklow was rolled gold
Between the trees that flagged us past
Like children waving welcome.
Whole valleys came out in a show of goodwill.
We drove on down in a royal progress.

New anecdotes were unpeeled, tossed like rind
Through the wound-down windows,
As if our lives too were bio-degradable,
Would return to a compost, renourish
Yet another crop of hardy adventures.

With darkness, drink. A hotel bar
In a square with a dash of Balkan decay,
A place that had seen better days
It never even knew were good. So into
Bare bulbs, urine scents, old rusty Player signs.

The six or so capped huddlers turned
To take us in, talk dropping off.
They took us for tourists in our city clothes.
Still we passed the test — or the excuse — for song
And someone led off Kelly from Killane.

The tune buckled like a sawblade
Under his belting strokes. The word *wizened*
Fitted him snugly as the shiny waistcoat
It seemed he'd worn forever. My nostrils still
Can wrinkle up his hum through the tang of stout.

Ballads overflowed like creamy heads.
Jokes, innuendo, jar, lashings of crack
Spilt on and then they started on Bing
And fifties hits, country and western,
Scraps of dated pop with tele-jingles last.

Rebel hillsides or soap opera both
Seemed the same, the raw hard stuff of song —
So what is wrong with that? Not much,
I think, except to know the difference
And just that one elates, the other saddens me.

And then our turn. You fetched your guitar
From the car and sang for them the song
You promised me you'd sing. It lay
Like layers of smoke across the air,
Contours unrolling as you'd written it.

I thought how like the long ellipse
Made by the blurring chords of your guitar
Were all the trade routes of our travels,
A map with two arterial roads being one
For that one lapsing second, like the strings.

We drove off into the leathery night
With invites to come back, ''you and
Your wife or whoever she is'', our open secret
Sensed, just as we knew their own unguarded one:
A world long open after closing time.

SLIM VOLUMES

An Irishman's pub is his castle.
Hedge-schooled in stout,
Who hasn't pigswilled till he puked?
Night after night the same again.
The fellowship of the high stool
Backslaps its failing wit,
Salves its conscience with smiles
That speak slim volumes.
Here all tragedy's a joke and a joke
Is tragedy if you're the butt of it.
Your point about the swan in Mallarmé?
Try Gogarty, the dons, and Yeats!
The convulsions of Vesuvius
Are nothing to the laughter of a literary man.
Nothing is lost on them. Yet they are lost,
The lost tribe of dribbling scribblers.
And again who, his liver mincemeat,
His head a kettledrum, throat
Dry as turfdust, hasn't felt the urge
To lurch and stagger after them?
Living? You hear them laugh, Living?
Living! Our barman can do that for us!

OUR GREATEST ASSET

Mick, Tom and Jim are law abiding lads.
Through no fault of their own
They are part of the army of the unemployed.

The Labour Exchange is a long dungeon.
Strangely, it reminds Tom of a slave market
He saw in an epic with Charlton Heston.

The dole, in a way, is a class of excursion,
A chance to run into people you were at school with.
You feel sorry for the clerks who have to stay there.

Three twenty odd is near seventy, which
Is not enough for a single man never mind three.
Still you can do something with it.

Jim's da has a colour set. The lads hire
The video from Lively Rentals Ltd.
They get a film a day and pull the curtains.

They are good lads, massgoing in this day and age,
And have never experimented with drugs.
Their hearts slither when the tape adjusts.

THE LAPPED WATERLINE

I.M. Brett Taylor 1943 – 1983

I found your old boat beached under the shade
Of tamarisk trees, sand sifting up the deck,
The cabin shuttered, fittings and lifeline frayed.
Here is your island grave, not a transatlantic

Cemetery of coffined rows under a lead-lined sky.
From here I watch the bay you used to sail,
Can nearly hear you start again some wry
Outlandish life-enhancing tale

That always made us listen, laugh — and love.
For what so grieved you there's no gift or cure
Like the lapped waterline your boat's above.
The once enriched feel keenly to be poor.

A LESSON IN PERSPECTIVE

After scaling the impossible wall
The cat burglar in the comic strip
Slips over the sill above the twinkling city,
Dissects the room with his pencil torch,
Unveils the safe behind the hinged picture.
Ear pressed to the purring ticks
He learns the secret of the tumblers
By silences in the notched maze.
The thick door suddenly swings
On searchlit nothing, no stacked wads
Or sparklers, only the four naked
Walls of stainless steel cell.
Through the slits in his mask
His mind almost loses its balance,
Struck by love's vertigo and the lines
Hurtling in to the vanishing point.

THE AGE OF ANYTHING

Will it be called the Age of anything?
''It's so terrible it's unthinkable.'' The same's
Been said of Auschwitz. Who'll edit the
Definitive Nuclear Anthology? I doubt if any
Huddler underground will feel compelled
To resurrect the Muse. Oddly, the arts
Need men more than the quoted obverse.
As you see, I can't think it too. Can God?
I can't begin. So here's a wisp of straw,
Epiphany of hayseed philosophy:
Around a farmhouse fire an old man said,
''Each new weapon they've invented they've
Tried out. Now they've better ones.
They won't rest easy.'' I feel we all feel that,
A slow black tumour at the back of the brain.
Who's not sick of our century's second childhood?
The old mass murderer playing for time,
History repeating itself in its senility.

SALT LAKE CITY, SANDYMOUNT

For Desmond Windle

Like bad actors in their tilted hats
And double-breasted suits
The two baby-faced Mormon missionaries
Set out at eight each morning
From their bedsit down the street.
Sometimes I nod to them.
They call me Sir.

Then around seven they slump home
Like job hunters back to the dole.
God knows what mockery and resentment
They meet on the doorsteps of this
Indifferent city. No one's work
Can bear too much rejection.

Shirtsleeved this summer's night they play
Some kind of baseball game without a bat
On the road under my window.
I can hear their shouts as they keep score.
The ball bounces into gardens,
Cars stop the play.
Suddenly heart-scalded and
Ashamed of feeling so akin to them
I almost love them in their lovelessness.

THE SKY AT NIGHT

The insomniac stars are sparking
In their loose connections.
One slips away in a long trajectory
Wavering in the flawed glass
Of the bedroom window. It takes
Ten minutes or minor age
To perish on a battery of chimney stacks.
Below, the garden is a charcoal sketch
Proportioned by the crossbarred panes.
Downstairs I brew tea wondering
If burnt out spy-in-the-sky or weather
Satellites spell kind or deadly portents
To dwindling tribes in Papua or the Amazon.
Or can Canaveral give birth to Bethlehem?

THE ANCHORITE

Up here in the condemned towerblocks
I am more self-sufficient than any islander.
The roof holds rainwater; migratory birds
Think they are too high for my traps.
I cook them on smashed woodwork
And keep warm. I shit in the liftshaft,
Which is a bit dangerous till you get the knack.
At dusk the city crinkles like a cooling engine,
Then police lights and sirens, *son et lumière.*
The social workers stay on the lower stories
Since the third corpse was found on the stairwell.
All in all I think this is the best place to be
Though I am exhausted trying to interpret
The wind's one-sided conversation with the world.

SNAKESKIN

Under a boulder
It lay like an S
As long as a belt
Translucent silver
The ghost of a snake

A shell of scales
Blunt arrowhead
Bulbous skull
I trembled to touch it
And when I did

It whipped alive
Leapt like a spring
Into a woven ring.
A shed skin
Is never truly dead.

LITTLE TOM THUMBSCREW

Little Tom Thumbscrew
Winds up his rack
A cat o'nine tails
Crisscrosses a back

Two terminals lead
From penis to tongue
Like a beast in the butcher's
A man is hamstrung

A human is sitting
Behind the white glare
Another is writhing
In a dentist's chair

Per grada ad idem
By steps to the same
A latinate motto
Curdles the brain

In an underground cell
A chamber is spun
If you heard the shot
It wasn't your turn.

THE CRANNOG DWELLERS

They built islands by sinking
Stones into a thorntree cage.
Capped the lot with earth,
Then huts and a stockade.

Under the water's puzzled skin
They laid a maze of stepping stones.

On our man-forsaken headlands
Aluminium saucers turn
Their Cyclops eyes.
They signal to the sunken silos.
For some acts of love and war
There is no retrieval system.

I prefer to think of the Crannog dwellers
Skipping across the lake
In a shower of stones.

THE DAM

The water hitches her flounced skirt
Against the hill's gross thigh.
Still something rankles in their coupling.

These valleys were hollowed for cloud and rain,
Not the twitch and glitter of silk and tweed.
There is an unease in the great barrage,

It seems so solid it must crack.
Dissatisfied, we drive back down
And boil its sterile waters for our tea.

THE DRUMMOND FUNERALS

Leaning on their trunks like laurelled pikes,
A guard of honour at a shallow grave,
The trees bow their heads at the top of the drive,
Incline to the solid house their last respects
Then twitch erect on the next shift of wind
As if summoned by the musquetry of crows.
Yet there they stay to watch another hearse
Squirt pebbles from its tyres into the ditch.

Lately I've come here only for funerals,
Pelting the dual-carriageway, then into by-ways
I half remember, St Bridgid's crossroads, hints
From that two-room school house, this hand-lettered shop
Until the house strides on its hill, slate-helmeted,
Flanked by the padded shoulders of its barns
And the tossed bouquet of an orchard.
The fields say simply: seed is permanence.

Some truck or combine's knocked a pier askew.
Cap doffed — by half — to the machine eye
It sentries the rucked lane. Does the car
Jolt just where a small boy found his father
One school morning? After a night out too many
My grandfather never quite made it home.
My father found the body. On the front room wall
I can see no carouser in the framed sepia

Nor glint of tolerance in his bride's composure.
The picture states the terms of their marriage
Like the provisions of Wyndham's Land Act
That confirmed their acres. Strong Farmer and Wife
Could caption them in textbook social history.
I hear his ringing heavy drinker's voice, her cold
Ripostes above the black Kilkenny mantlepiece
Distilled into their children's guarded tones.

It seems as if they were felled by a fusillade,
A scattered volley nailing them across a decade,
Each year St. Mullin's graveyard opening its gates
To brother or sister until the family plot
Gained on the family, the quiet house now quieter,
The air drying along the bedroom corridor
To the old apple smell of celibacy and age.
Childlessness shells the heart of a house.

This was always a farm for the latest methods
Where new strains of breed prospered among
Bright rumbling harvesters and antiseptic steel.
The land itself was their collective child.
John, carefully dealing in yields and herds
Could have deliberated in a merchant bank
And Katie run a convent boarding school —
I could name them in a litany with their gifts

To match the formal version slit into stone
On crosses and slanted slabs, Patrick
versus Pat, Lizzie, Elizabeth, Katie, Catherine,
The same names belled again each generation
Back two centuries. Lichen lines and shades
Counties across the incised names like the blank map
Of Ireland they filled in at school. The trade routes
Of my life seem distant as Tashkent,

My preoccupations far fetched as the Crusades,
Irrelevant as silk or spice, spurious exotica
Against the telling test of work, the only ethic.
Even prayer was a relaxtion, illness a dodge
Till death proved it genuine. The rest is hearsay.
These filaments twined round my father's life
Like slow lake weeds. I can't pretend I am not
Netted too in the long undertow of ancestry.

THE TRIBAL TERRITORIES

Small placards said, ''The Government of Pakistan
Is not responsible for your safety if you leave the road.''
We stopped for soft drinks in a border town
And let the diesel cool. Drugs and duty-free
Cassettes, no, we didn't want. But I bought
A brass button with an embossed harp
From a man squatting in a circle of junk.
It was there I saw the old Pathan with his bandolier
And antique Lee Enfield. He looked ninety
And was barely able to lug the thing around.
I felt like saying, ''Look here, let me take that.
You're not fit to be in charge of it.
You'll do yourself damage,
Never mind anyone else.''
Needless to say I said nothing.
The Landrover gnashed on up the Khyber Pass
Past the crests of old regiments cut in the rock.

That same year in Belfast, in the ''Catholic
Enclave of Short Strand'' I saw
A boy soldier with an automatic rifle
And a two-way radio strapped to his back
Quiver in terror as much as his aerial,
Eyeballs flicking like marbles about the roadblock.
I felt like getting out of the car and saying
''Look here, let me. . . .''

REMEMBERING MANOLI

The longsleeved windmills
Signal like sailors
Across the hull of the valley.
But it's the abandoned mills,
Dismasted, shelled
By time that will not take
Dried mud for mortar
That are the unmapped benchmarks
For Manoli and his mules
Heaving cement up to our house
Past the three threshing circles
Sewn like old drachmae
Into the pleated hill.
Nor was your currency
Quite negotiable either
At the mind's full rates.
A short-change of genes
Left you gentle if lacking
The counterfeit of normality.
Your greetings were fresh
As the laundered shirt
You sported for festivals
Though your house was dark
And pungent as the tawny wine
You fermented alone,
Wifeless, deserted to mind
Your daft son who sang
Church rituals and tele-ads
From the tops of trees
All through the siesta.

And when that television
Went on the blink
We went up and found
A woolly nest of mice
Breeding among the valves.
Your death was awful.
One night you threw a fit
And I helped you home
As you lurched like a drunk
Though you hadn't a drop.
We said, *one day that will*
Happen at the lip of a well.
So it did. When I stare
Down the cobbled tunnel
I think of you slipping
Like a loaded windlass
And see your face
Submerged in the mirror
Mouthing dumb screams
Through the rubble wall
The clouds built over you.

THE OLD FLAME

A poem slides into its shape
Like a glass of red wine spilt
On a shelf of ribcaged rock —
On rosé sandstone, say.

Tentacles of vein
Seek their own level,
Nudge back along canals
To a bloodorange pool

That dries in the dipping sun.
And the stain slowly becoming
A perfect match for the rock?
Is the old chameleon experience.

But what of the blaze in the lens
Of the bladed sliver of glass?
Only love, the sly fire-raiser,
All set to engulf the house.